Stories, sayings, and scriptures to Encourage and Insp

"拥抱·爱"系列双语典藏读物

hugs

TM

for

those in love

U0105713

love

两人一世界

Ron and Lyn Rose
LeAnn Weiss

著

杨 芳 译

安徽科学技术出版社

HOWARD BOOKS
PUBLISHING CO.

[皖] 版贸登记号：1208543

图书在版编目（CIP）数据

拥抱·爱. 两人一世界:英汉对照/(美)罗恩,(美)罗斯
(Rose,L.)著；杨芳译. —合肥：安徽科学技术出版社,
2009.1
ISBN 978-7-5337-4262-1

Ⅰ. 拥… Ⅱ. ①罗…②罗…③杨… Ⅲ. ①英语-汉语-
对照读物②故事-作品集-美国-现代 Ⅳ. H319.4：I

中国版本图书馆 CIP 数据核字(2008)第 198279 号

拥抱·爱. 两人一世界:英汉对照
(美)罗恩 (美)罗斯(Rose,L.) 著 杨芳 译

出 版 人：黄和平
责任编辑：李瑞生
封面设计：朱 婧
出版发行：安徽科学技术出版社(合肥市政务文化新区圣泉路 1118 号
出版传媒广场,邮编：230071)
电 话：(0551)3533330
网 址：www. ahstp. net
E - mail：yougoubu@sina. com
经 销：新华书店
排 版：安徽事达科技贸易有限公司
印 刷：安徽新华印刷股份有限公司
开 本：787×1240 1/32
印 张：5.5
字 数：71 千
版 次：2009 年 1 月第 1 版 2009 年 1 月第 1 次印刷
印 数：6 000
定 价：16.00 元

(本书如有印装质量问题,影响阅读,请向本社市场营销部调换)

给爱一个归宿
——出版者的话

身体语言是人与人之间最重要的沟通方式,而身体失语已让我们失去了很多明媚的"春天",为什么不可以给爱一个形式?现在就转身,给你爱的人一个发自内心的拥抱,你会发现,生活如此美好!

肢体的拥抱是爱的诠释,心灵的拥抱则是情感的沟通,彰显人类的乐观坚强、果敢执著与大爱无疆。也许,您对家人、朋友满怀缱绻深情却羞于表达,那就送他一本《拥抱·爱》吧。一本书,七个关于真爱的故事;一本书,一份荡涤尘埃的"心灵七日斋"。一个个叩人心扉的真实故事,一句句震撼心灵的随笔感悟,从普通人尘封许久的灵魂深处走出来,在洒满大爱阳光的温情宇宙中尽情抒写人性的光辉!

"拥抱·爱"(Hugs)系列双语典藏读物是"心灵鸡汤"的姊妹篇,安徽科学技术出版社与美国出版巨头西蒙舒斯特携手倾力打造,旨在把这套深得美国读者青睐的畅销书作为一道饕餮大餐,奉献给中国的读者朋友们。

每本书附赠CD光盘一张,纯正美语配乐朗诵,让您在天籁之音中欣赏精妙美文,学习地道发音。

世界上最遥远的距离,不是树枝无法相依,而是相互凝望的星星却没有交会的轨迹。

"拥抱·爱"系列双语典藏读物,助您倾吐真情、启迪心智、激扬人生!

一本好书一生财富,今天你拥抱了吗?

Contents

CHAPTER ONE Bringing Out the Best ········· 1

1. 做到最好 ············· 3

CHAPTER TWO Appreciating Differences ··· 25

2. 欣赏迥别 ············· 27

CHAPTER THREE Activating Romance ········· 49

3. 制造浪漫 ············· 51

CHAPTER FOUR Marking Milestones ········· 73

4. 注重拐点 ············· 75

CHAPTER FIVE Choosing to Be Best Friends ··· 97

5. 愿做挚友 ············· 99

CHAPTER SIX Investing in Others ··········· 121

6. 关爱他人 ············· 123

CHAPTER SEVEN Finding Forgiveness ······ 145

7. 寻求谅解 ············· 147

Of all the

earthly music, that

which reaches

farthest into heaven

is the beating of

a truly loving heart.

—Henry Ward Beecher

在所有尘世的音乐中,能悠远至天堂的唯有爱的律动。

亨利 华德 比琪

$\mathscr{T}$hree little words,

"*I love you,*"

are the words that

topple empires, shape

destinies, make men

and women risk their lives

and unite millions of couples

in holy matrimony

every year.

What power is in those words!

—Nancy Corbett Cole

有三个简单的字

"我爱你"

可以颠覆世界，

创造姻缘，让成千上万的男男

女女奋不顾身走进神圣婚烟。

这三个字里孕育着

多么伟大的能量！

——南西·考波特·卡尔

CHAPTER ONE

*Bringing Out
the Best*

1

做到最好

$\mathcal{I}$ve caused you to leave your parents to join your lives together forever. You're no longer two, but one. You're able to love because I first loved you! Don't just love with words; demonstrate your love with action and in truth. Learn the secret of being content in every situation.

Uniting You,

your god of peace

—from Mark 10:7–8; 1 John 4:19; 3:18; Philippians 4:12

我让你们离开父母，把你们的生命永远结合在一起。你们不再是两个人，从此合二为一。你们能够相爱，首先是我的眷顾，不要是口头上说"我爱你"，而是用行动和真心相爱。请相信这个在任何情况下都能让人满意的秘密。

——伴随你们的和平之神

Love is a gift that takes a lifetime to un-
wrap. Just when we think we've figured it out, we
discover something new that changes everything. As
we grow older and more willing to live in the pre-
sent—without feeling trapped by the past or worried
about the future—we realize this gift has many dimen-
sions. There's a sensual side; an affectionate and romantic side;   a compassionate and tender side;   a
funloving, surprising side; a strategic, problem-solving
side; and a practical side; just to name a few. The
gift of love has many components.

All lifelong, intimate relationships are built
on the promise to be a giver of this gift. The
mystery is that the more love we give,
the more we have to give—the supply
continues to grow, unendingly. We
receive love even when we
don't deserve it.   When the

doors are closed and the lights are off, we all have our share of undesirable habits and quirky secrets. Lifelong love, grace-love, what the Bible calls *agape* love, is the gift of seeing the best in each other, regardless.

This kind of love is rare, and we must experience it before we can give it.

This gift of love refuses to label or limit others. It inspires and encourages and lifts others, whether we feel like it or not. Instead of controlling and dominating a lover, it finds ways to see the good and bring out the best in spite of the circumstances.

This may sound unrealistic. It is, to those who have not experienced it. To Christians, however, it is a reflection of God's love.

爱是需要用一生的时间去了解的

礼物，当我们以为自己已经彻悟时，却又发现一些

新的可以改变一切的深意。随着年龄的增长，我们更愿

意活在当下。不回忆过去的艰辛，不顾虑将来的命运。我

们知道，这个礼物具有许多含义。有世俗情欲的含义，有

挚爱浪漫的含义，有温柔关爱的含义，有开心惊讶的含

义，有克服难题的含义，还有许多其他实际的意义，

只不过有着不同的新名称。爱这个礼物蕴藏着多

种深意。

我们的一生，美满而甜蜜的关系建立在

给予这种礼物的承诺上。很神奇

的是，我们给予的爱越多，越

想给予，所给予的爱

会不断增长，永

不停息。

我们甚至会收到超值的爱的回礼。

关上门,关上灯,我们都有一些不好的习惯和难以启齿的秘密。终生的爱、优雅的爱又被叫做"盲目的爱",它是一种不顾一切、只能看到对方优点的爱。

这种爱是非常珍贵的,我们只有经历过才可以给予。

这种爱的礼物不附带任何条件,让人吃惊,给人鼓舞,令人兴奋。它不是用来控制和支配所爱的人的礼物,它是竭尽所能发现所爱的人的美好的一面并使之尽善尽美的礼物。

对那些没有经历过的人,这听起来多么不可思议,然而,它与天地同在。

当我们的爱情
在上帝心中诞生，
它们会展现我们最
好的一面，因为是
爱孕育了它们。

——唐·莱辛

When our
relationships are
born in the heart
of god, they bring
out the best in
us, for they are
nurtured by love.

—Don Lessin

"父亲，你有什么秘诀可以使
你和母亲的爱如此深厚持
久？请告诉我。"

"Dad, what's your secret?
you and Mom have
always been so much in
love. Please tell me."

Mom's Little Secret

The ceremony was arranged, the rehearsal festivities had gone well, and Kate's dad was staying up late, as usual. He sat in his favorite chair on the deck, looking up toward the stars but not seeing any of them. It had been a long day, and the anticipation of Kate's wedding was playing in his mind like a film from long ago. As he was enjoying the moment, the door opened, interrupting his reverie.

It was Kate—an unexpected but pleasant interruption.

"What's up, kid?" he asked.

"Can I sit here for just a bit?" she asked, ignoring his question.

"Of course," Dad responded, making room. "This reminds me of when you were a little girl and you'd come out here when you couldn't sleep. You know, everything will be different after tomorrow, and that's the way it should be. I couldn't be happier for you and David."

For a bit, they reviewed the day, laughing over the hilarious family video they'd watched at the rehearsal dinner. They also shed a tear or two as both realized this would be their last night together as "Dad and his little girl." Their relationship was about to change in some indescribable, unexperienced way.

After a period of silence, Kate asked, "Dad, what's your secret? You and Mom have always been so much in love. Please tell me."

"Kate," her Dad confessed, "it's not my secret— it's your mom's. From the day we met, she has made it her life's goal to bring out the best in me."

"What do you mean?" Kate asked.

"When we began dating, she introduced me as the last of the grand gentlemen. Your mom made it easy for me to be a grand gentleman to her. I courted her as if she were a queen; all I desired was to win her heart. After we married, she bragged to her friends that I was the best listener in the world, that I really understood her. And she helped me learn to listen, to listen beyond the words, to listen for the sake of listening. It was tough for me. It took a lot of time. I wanted a shortcut, some way to solve the problems and fix whatever was broken. But she just wanted me to listen. It seemed strange, but as she gently taught me, I really learned how to listen."

"Didn't you feel like she was trying to change you all the time?" Kate quizzed. "What happened when you didn't measure up?"

He leaned up in his chair and looked deep into his daughter's eyes. "Kate, your mom loves me, regardless. That's what we promised to each other on our wedding day. She doesn't require me to be better in order to be loved; she loves me in spite of my failures, not just when I am good or because I am good."

"I'm not sure I understand," Kate declared. "Are you talking about grace or love?"

"Both," Dad answered. "They're sort of the same thing. Love makes you a dispenser of grace. Your mom doesn't love me because I love her or when I love her; she loves me because she promised to love me — in spite of my failures, struggles, or stubbornness."

"You know, Dad," Kate affirmed, "You do the same thing for Mom."

"I've tried to," he answered.

Kate reached out, took her dad's hand, and slipped into his lap. She hugged him like she had when she was a child, only this time was even more special. It marked a moment of truth between father and daughter that would outlive them both.

After a bit, Dad said, "You know, all my life I've been a better person because your mother loved me, and now you have the opportunity to help David become a better man too."

"I will always love you, Dad. You and Mom have given me more than you will ever know. David doesn't realize it yet, but he's going to be the best husband ever."

Kate left her dad sitting in his chair on the deck, looking toward the stars but not seeing any of them.

妈妈的小秘密

　　婚礼即将举行，欢乐的喜宴已过，凯特的父亲像往常一样很晚还没有睡。他坐在阳台上自己喜爱的椅子上，仰望天上的星星，但其实什么也没有看到。这一天很长，凯特就要到来的婚礼像放电影一样反复在他脑海中预演着，他正沉浸在这幸福时刻，忽然门开了，打断了他的幻想。

　　来的是凯特，是很意外却很高兴见到的人。

　　"什么事，孩子？"他问。

　　凯特没有回答，却说："我可以在这儿坐一会儿吗？"

父亲往旁边挪了挪说："当然可以，这让我想起以前，你还是个小女孩时，如果睡不着，就会到这儿来，不是吗？过了明天，一切都不一样了，这是必然的。我真为你和大卫高兴。"

他们一起回顾了白天的事，全家人一起欢庆、笑闹，共同观看喜庆的家庭录像。当意识到这将是作为"爸爸和小女儿"共度的最后一个晚上，他们还是流了眼泪。他们之间将要变成一种难以描述的、从未经历过的关系。

静了一会后，凯特问爸爸："爸爸，你们有什么秘密吗，你和妈妈总是那么相爱，告诉我吧！"

爸爸很肯定地告诉女儿："凯特，我没有秘密，秘密来自你妈妈，从我们相遇的第一天起，她一生的目标就是让我更加完美。"

"什么意思？"凯特问。

"当我们开始约会时，她向别人介绍我，言语间仿佛我就是一个了不起的绅士。你妈妈让我不自觉地以绅士的态度对待她，向她献殷勤，拿她当皇后，渴望得到她的心。结婚后，她对朋友吹嘘，说我是世界上最好的聆听者，是最最理解她的人。是她帮助我学会聆听，听那些言外之意，养成喜爱听的习惯。这些对我来说并不容易，我用了很长一段时间。遇到要解决的问题和矛盾，我总想找捷径。但她只想让我听，是不是很怪。但她一直温柔地教我，我真正学会了如何去听。"

凯特追问："你不觉得妈妈一直想要改变你吗？当你达不到要求的时候，会怎么样呢？"

父亲往后靠在椅子上，眼睛盯着女儿的双眸："凯特，你妈妈爱我，并没有什么条件，我们在结婚那一天就相互承诺了，为了爱，她不会要求我变得更好，她爱我包括我的不足，不是当我表现得好或因为我优秀才会爱我。"

"我不是很明白，"凯特说，"您是在说礼貌地对待彼此还是在说爱情呢？"

"两者皆有，"父亲答道，"它们其实是同一件事，因为爱一个人，你才会善待他(她)。你的妈妈不是因为我爱她或是当我爱她时，她才会爱我，她爱我是因为承诺过爱我，无论我处在失败、竞争还是艰难的时刻,她都一样爱我。"

凯特很肯定地说:"你知道吗?爸爸,你对妈妈也是一样的。"

"我一直努力这么做。"父亲回答。

凯特伸出手,握住爸爸的手,依偎到他膝前,像小时候那样拥抱着他。这一刻,多么奇妙,这一刻预示着父亲和女儿之间真诚的情义长存。

过了一会儿,父亲说,"要知道,因为你妈妈的爱,我一生都是个好人。现在,你也有机会帮助大卫成为一个好人。"

"我永远爱你,爸爸,你和妈妈给了我连你们自己都想象不到的、那么多的帮助。大卫现在还不了解,但他一定会成为我最好的丈夫。"

凯特离开了她的父亲,而他还坐在阳台的椅子上,仰望着天空的星星,却什么也没有看到。

Reflections . .

What secrets have you observed in other marriages or your own that have helped love grow?

CHAPTER TWO

Appreciating

Differences

2

欣賞迴別

Let love be your motivation. Be completely humble and gentle, practicing patience as you bear with one another in love. When you accept one another just as Christ accepted you, you bring praise to Me. I'll give you a spirit of unity between you as you follow My Son together, cheering each other on to love and good deeds.

Love,

your god of Encouragement

—from 1 Corinthians 16:14; Ephesians 4:2; Romans 15:5–7;
Hebrews 10:24

让爱成为你们的动力，在相互间的爱中更加的谦恭、文雅，有耐心。当你们接受了对方，那么上帝也接受了你们。你们赞美了我，我会给你们结合的力量，让你们跟随我的儿子为爱和爱的成果互相喝彩。

——你们的鼓励之神

In a relationship, we bring many differences to the table. Some of them are quickly noticeable and wonderfully appreciated; others, however, lie in the background, annoying and distracting us. These differences have the potential to eat away at a relationship, killing it with resentment and frustration, or they can energize a relationship, taking it to new worlds of adventure and new levels of trust.

Do any of these sound familiar?

—He avoids failure and seeks independence; she avoids isolation and seeks intimacy.

—She wants to talk, just to talk; he'll talk when there is a problem to solve or something to fix.

—She quickly stops and asks for directions, even before she's lost; he feels that asking for directions is a sign of weakness.

—She has a clean desk; he has a roll top.

—He's working to recover from a turbulent childhood; she's living in a fairy-tale world.

—She grows spiritually by becoming involved in every

church ministry; he grows spiritually by escaping to the mountains for some time alone with God.

—He is a conservative Republican; she hasn't told him, but she didn't even vote in the last election.

—She talks in order to sort out her thoughts; he won't speak until he has thought it all out.

—He thrives on risk; she avoids risk.

Our differences form a path to mutual understanding. We can walk that path and learn to appreciate each other, or we can complain about the conditions and never even begin the journey. Learn to embrace and celebrate your differences.

The combination of our differences makes us unique. After all, no couple in the world has our assortment of differences.

We were created with these differences for a reason—to shape, refine, admonish, enrich, and balance each other. We transform each other as though we become the hands of God. We cannot become our best without our counterparts.

在人与人的关系中，有许多不同
的观点，有些是显而易见的，非常容易对待，而
另一些却藏匿在背后，让我们苦恼、心烦。这样的潜在
分歧会渐渐蚕食掉和睦的关系，让我们感觉到怨恨和挫
败。但也能为我们的关系增添新的活力，带领我们进入一
个新的世界，创造出新的忠诚。

下面这些你听说过吗？

——他要走出挫败感，争取独立；而她却要摆脱孤
独，寻找亲密。

——她想要与人交谈，只要交谈；而他却在碰到
需要解决的问题和处理事情时才会与人交谈。

——她在迷失方向前，就会停下来向别人询
问方向；而他则认为向别人打听方向是无能的
表现。

——她有一张简洁的书桌；而他的
书桌是拉盖的。

——他正在努力地从喧闹
的儿童时代中苏醒；而她还
沉溺在童话世界里。

——她的精神
世界伴随着各
种各样的
教

堂；而他常常一个人溜进深
山,寻找与自然独处的时光。

——他是保守党支持者；而她虽然没有告诉
他,但大选时她都没去投票。

——她与人交谈,是为了做出决定;而他做出决定后
才会告诉别人。

——他爱冒险;而她却躲避危险。

我们有这么多分歧，但它可以形成一条通往相互理
解的路。

我们一起走在路上,就要学会欣赏对方,否则只能
指责环境,永不出发。让我们拥抱分歧,为分歧欢呼
吧。

把我们的分歧结合起来会让我们很独特。
世界上没有任何两对夫妻的分歧是完全一样
的。

这些分歧改造了我们。因为在分歧
中我们相互塑造、修炼、劝告、提高
和比照。

我们是上帝的左手和右
手，我们互相改造着对
方。没有对方,我们不
可能变得更完
美。

爱以相互包容、相
互提升的方式，在两
个相爱的人之间，不
断升华。

——费利克斯·阿德勒

*Love is the
expansion of two
natures in such a
fashion that
each includes the
other, each is
enriched by the
other.*

—Felix Adler

Most of their best talks took place when they traveled late at night.

他们的倾心交谈多数发生在夜间旅行时。

What a Strange Thing to Say

On an evening nearing his one-month wedding anniversary, Jim was relaxing in his first new
piece of furniture, the recliner—the "man" chair.
Finally, he felt like a real grownup. However, not
everything was complete; the greatest invention of
the modern world—the TV remote control—had not
yet found its way to Jim's living room.

Carol was in the kitchen fiddling with
something, and Jim called to her to ask for a glass
of tea. If he worked it right, she would function as

his remote control, and Jim wouldn't have to get up. His plan was to get her to change the channel on her way back to the kitchen.

But Carol evidently had a different idea. Handing the tea to Jim, she preempted his request with, "It's time to take out the garbage, hon."

She caught Jim off guard, and he forgot to ask her to change the channel.

Jim thought, *What a strange thing to say*. Why would she tell him what she was about to do? He didn't make an announcement every time he washed the car or mowed the lawn. Then, Carol repeated herself, only this time with a louder voice and a touch of frustration.

"Did you hear me? It's time to take out the garbage! "

That's her job, Jim thought to himself. *She's violating the natural order of things. Men do the outside stuff, and women do the inside stuff. My mother took care of the garbage in the house, and my dad dealt with it outside. That's the way it's sup-posed to be.*

Not only was Carol requesting something un-natural, she was already turning into his mother. She was telling Jim what to do and when to do it. He suddenly saw his future unfold before him: He was going to be henpecked the rest of his life.

Why can't she just keep quiet? Jim thought. *I'll take out her garbage in a little bit—when it's my idea.*

But this time she meant business: "Jim, get out of that chair and take care of this garbage! "

Jim took out the garbage, but he didn't like it, and he sulked for a week.

This pattern was repeated over and over again for months, until Jim and Carol returned to their hometown for Christmas vacation. As strange as it felt to spend the night in Carol's old bed with her parents in the next room, something else seemed even more strange. Jim noticed that Carol's dad had evidently missed the outside/inside job-description bulletin. Each night he made the rounds through the house gathering trash, and each night he took all the trash outside. No wonder Carol expected Jim to take care of the garbage. Her dad took out the family trash daily,thus sabotaging Jim's idea of the natural division of labor.

Once the holidays ended, Jim and Carol headed home. It was a long trip, but to save the cost of a motel room, they decided to drive all night. About 3:00 A.M., they were talking about all sorts of stuff, just to keep each other awake. In fact, most of their best talks took place when they traveled late at night. It was dark, and Jim didn't have to look into Carol's eyes, so he could talk about anything.

"I guess you've noticed that I've had an attitude problem about the garbage," Jim opened.

"I know," she responded.

"Well, I saw your dad doing the garbage detail, and now I understand why you think I should take it out. I've just never considered the garbage my job. Don't get me wrong; it's no big deal. I just don't want to be told to do it. You're my wife, not my mother," Jim explained.

Then, he added, almost as an afterthought, "I just want it to be my idea, okay?"

"Sure," Carol said, "I can live with that."

For a while neither talked; then the conversation moved on to hunger, and they decided to search for somewhere to stop for a snack.

A couple of days after Jim and Carol returned home, the garbage stacked up pretty high under the sink. With her newfound knowledge of Jim's views on the garbage, Carol stood at the doorway to the kitchen and asked, "Honey, is it your idea to take out the garbage yet?"

"It sure is," Jim answered. "It's my idea to do the garbage detail at the next commercial."

It worked for them!

陌生的语言

结婚一个月的纪念日很快就要到了，吉米轻松地靠在他的新家具躺椅上——那是男人的椅子。现在，他终于感到自己真正长大了，是个男人了。然而，美中不足的是，他在周围没有找到那个可称为现代社会最伟大的发明的东西——电视遥控器。

卡罗正在厨房里忙着什么，吉米让她给自己送杯水。如果可能的话，她可以充当遥控器，吉米就不用自己站起来了，他想让卡罗回厨房时顺便替他换一下频道。

可是卡罗很显然有自己的想法，她把茶递给吉米后，抢先说："该倒垃圾了，亲爱的。"

吉米愣住了，忘了让她换频道那事。

吉米觉得她的话很奇怪，很陌生。

她自己要做什么，干吗要告诉他。比如吉米要洗车，要整理草坪也没有事先通知她呀。

可是，卡罗重复着那句话，只是这次声音更大，好像有些不满意。

"听见了吗？该倒垃圾了。"

吉米想，倒垃圾该是她的事呀，她好像违反了男主外、女主内的自然规律。我妈妈就负责倒垃圾，爸爸负责外面的事。这样才是正确的。

卡罗不光会提出一些违反常规的问题，甚至快变成他的妈妈了。她总是告诉吉米要做什么，什么时候去做。这让吉米突然想到了自己的将来，以后会不会得"气管炎"（妻管严）。

吉米很懊恼，她不能不说话吗，如果我自己高兴，也可以帮她倒垃圾啊。

然而，这次她不只是简单地说说，是当真的："吉米，不要光坐着，把这些垃圾倒了！"

吉米把拉圾拿出去了，但他很不情愿，气了一个星期。

几个月来，这种情况重复了一次又一次。直到那一天，吉米和卡罗回到家乡过圣诞节。晚上卡罗的父母住在隔壁的房间，吉米和卡罗住在卡罗原来的房间。吉米感到很陌生。有些事情让吉米感到更加不习惯。吉米注意到卡罗的父亲很明显违反了内、外分工的原则。每天晚上他都会各个房间巡查一遍，收集各房垃圾并丢到外面去。所以，卡罗叫吉米倒垃圾一点也不奇怪。她爸爸就每天倒家里的垃圾。她对吉米有关内、外分工的说法不满也是可想而知的。

度假结束后，吉米和卡罗准备回家，路程很远，为了节省汽车旅馆的费用，他们决定连夜开车回家。凌晨三点左右，他们谈起了许多事情,以免打瞌睡。事实上,在他们深夜回家的路上,他们进行了他们之间最有价值的交谈,周围很黑,吉米看不清卡罗的眼睛,因而可以畅所欲言。

"我猜,你已经意识到我对倒垃圾这件事的态度了,"吉米开始说道。

"我知道,"卡罗答道。

"我看到你爸爸收拾垃圾的事,现在我明白了,你为什么让我倒垃圾,我从不认为这应该是我的工作。不要怪我,这不是什么大事。我只不过不愿被你支使着去做。你是我妻子,不是我妈妈。"吉米解释说。接着,仿佛思考后的决定,他补充说:"我就是想应该是我自己主动去做,明白吗?"

"当然,"卡罗说,"我也这样想。"

稍停了一会儿后,两人都渴望继续交谈,他们决定停车,找个地方休息一会。

吉米和卡罗回家后,过了几天,水池下面的垃圾堆了起来，卡罗想起吉米有关垃圾的观点，站在厨房的门口问道："亲爱的,你是主动要倒垃圾吗？"

"当然,"吉米答道:"是我自己要把收拾垃圾当做下一项工作的。"

这就是他们的相处之道。

Reflections . . .

$\mathcal{W}$hat "strange things" did you or your spouse bring to your marriage?   What have you learned about compromise and give-and-take?

_____

_____

_____

_____

_____

_____

_____

_____

_____

_____

_____

_____

_____

CHAPTER THREE

Activating
Romance

③

制造浪漫

Walk in love. Remember, love is patient and kind. It's not self-seeking or easily angered. Love always protects, always trusts, always hopes, and always perseveres. Be kind and compassionate to each other, forgiving each other's shortcomings just like Christ forgave you.

Compassionately,

your Heavenly father

—from 2 John 1:6;1 Corinthians 13:4–7;Ephesians 4:32

爱中漫步，过程曲折，爱要有耐心，爱要有情义。爱不是自我寻觅，爱不是生闷气。爱始终需要保护，需要诚实、希望和坚定不移，相互间的爱需要注入友情、同情和谅解。

——爱你的天父

Dozens of roses, alluring environments, candlelight dinners—these do not define romance. It cannot be measured in dollars spent or gifts received. Romance is the unexpected escape from the stresses of life. It's an intimate message that speaks of value and importance. In short, it refocuses and energizes a relationship.

A marriage without romance is dull, dominated by routine and scheduled by boredom. Marriage was designed from the beginning to preserve romance, not eliminate it. We are never too old to rekindle our efforts at romance. Little surprises can make a big difference: Hold hands while you walk. Call each other during the day. Go out for a Coke or a cup of coffee. Send a card or a letter that describes your love. Serve together in a ministry that focuses on helping those less fortunate than you. Watch an old movie together. Organize your pictures together.

It takes a little planning to keep romance alive year

after year. And those plans must translate into action. Good intentions don't count. We have to write the notes and slip them into the glove box. We have to call the hotel and make the reservations. We have to order the flowers, send the cards, take the walks, buy the chocolate, build the fire, draw the bath. Only when we actually do these things do they turn into romance.

Romance is our most effective method for communicating feelings. When we take romantic action, we communicate our love, even if we don't have the words to describe those feelings.

Knowing we are loved is not enough. Saying the words, "I love you," is not enough. We long to feel we are loved. Romance sends that feeling to the heart. It doesn't matter what it costs or what others think, as long as that heart message is sent and received. When we feel loved, we feel valuable, needed, special, extraordinary. Amazing, isn't it? Romance is not an option.

千百枝玫瑰，诱人的氛围和绚烂的烛光晚餐，都不能定义为浪漫。浪漫不能用花费的金钱、收到的礼物来衡量，浪漫是摆脱生活重压后的轻松。浪漫传递着珍贵和重要的信息。简而言之，浪漫更新着我们之间的关系，为之增加活力。

缺乏浪漫的婚姻是日常事务的消磨，是伴随着厌倦的度日。婚姻从一开始就意味着珍藏浪漫，而不是排斥浪漫。无论我们到了什么年龄都应鼓起浪漫的勇气。

小小的惊喜可以带来巨大的改变。手拉手散步，电话聊天，一起喝可乐和咖啡，互相赠送爱的信件和卡片，共同为同一目的工作来帮助那些比自己更不幸的人。一同去看老电影，一起整理照片等都可激起浪漫的火花。

长久地保持浪漫不需要过多的

　　　　筹划，而应该付诸行动。只有愿望
还不够。要记录下来珍藏，要打电话预订旅社，
要订购鲜花，要寄送贺卡，要去散步，要买巧克力，要建
造壁炉，要设计浴室。只有实实在在地做这些事，才会带
来浪漫。

　　浪漫是情感交流最有效的方法，当我们进行浪漫的
行动时，我们传递着爱意，尽管我们并没有用语言表
达。

　　了解我们的爱，用语言说"我爱你"是远远不
够的，我们渴望爱的感觉。浪漫把这种感觉种
在我们心里。无论结果如何，无论他人的
想法，只要心中还有爱的信息，我们
就能感觉到爱，感觉珍惜，感觉
被需要，感觉专一，感觉
非凡，感觉惊喜。浪
漫是唯一
的。

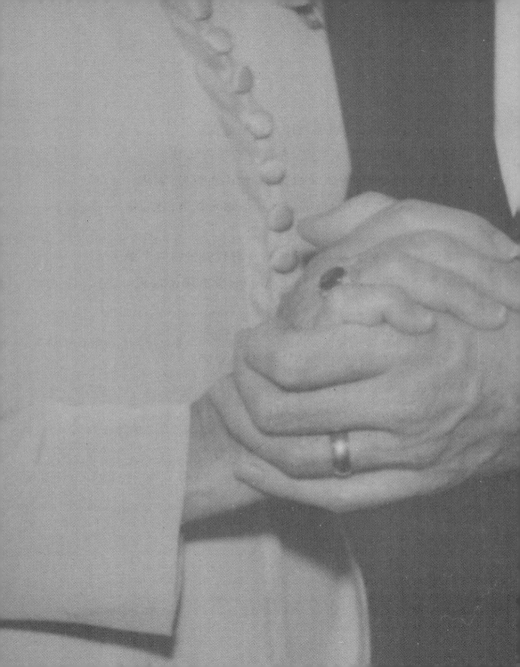

爱是心灵深处对
被了解和被原谅的永
久渴望。

——亨利·范·代克

*For love is
but the heart's
immortal thirst to
be completely
known and all
forgiven.*

—Henry Van Dyke

他喜欢炫耀他的新
车,但是到目前为止,他
从未给别人机会来驾驭
他自己的梦想。

*He loved to show off his
new car, but so far, he
had given no one else
the opportunity to
drive his dream.*

The Note Had Her Name on It

Michael had finally been able to buy his dream car. The kids were grown and on their own. Kristen's car was only two years old and in great shape. He had needed a new car, so why not go for the dream?

The '65 Mustang was in "better-than-new" condition. Granted, it didn't have all the electronics and fancy new gadgets, but it was a classic; Michael felt young and cool driving it around town and back and forth to work. He lived for the weekends when he and Kristen could cruise the countryside.

Of course, he kept his pride and joy sparkling. Whenever he had a spare moment, he spent it in the garage tinkering, polishing, and admiring his dream car. He loved to show it off, but so far, he had given no one else the opportunity to drive his dream.

But one afternoon, Kristen had to do some last-minute shopping for a party they planned to throw that evening. Her car was still in the shop because some out-of-stock computer chip had to be shipped from the West Coast.

When she'd asked Michael to take her to the market for the stuff she needed, his response had nearly stopped her heart. Throwing her his keys, he'd called, "You take my car. I've got to finish the lawn."

"Oh,no! " she'd shrieked. "What if something happens?"

"Honey, it's okay! You'll do fine," he'd returned.

Kristen had reluctantly gotten into the car and carefully driven to the market. After she'd gotten everything on her list, the bagger helped her put her sacks in the trunk.

"Nice car," he volunteered as he closed the trunk.

"It's my husband's," Kristen said as she carefully started the dream car and drove off. She was only two blocks from home when she looked down for just a moment to change the radio station. At that instant a dog ran into the street, and the driver of the pickup in front of her slammed on his brakes to avoid the animal. She stood on the brakes and swerved to the right, but it was too late.

She'll never forget the sound of crunching metal as the front left fender clipped the unyielding truck bumper. No one was hurt, not even the dog. But

Kristen was in hysterics.

"Michael! Michael! He'll never forgive me," she cried.

All she could do was sit there and sob. The driver of the pickup truck asked if she was hurt.

"You can't imagine how much I'm hurt," she cried.

"Do you need an ambulance?" he asked.

Finally getting a little control, she shook her head and responded, "Not now, but I may when my husband sees his car."

The truck driver introduced himself as Mr. Dunn. After looking over the damage, he assured her that she could still drive the car, but he needed to get her insurance information.

Kristen opened the glove box for the insurance papers. The small compartment held only a plastic protective envelope. Inside she found all the necessary insurance and registration papers—and a folded piece of notebook paper with her name on it. She quickly handed the insurance papers to Mr. Dunn.

"Here's what you need," she said.

Then, without another word, she turned her attention to the piece of paper with her name on it. She couldn't open it fast enough. She wondered what it could be. It didn't take long to read. She was speechless, and her tears were unstoppable.

"Are you sure you're all right?" Mr. Dunn asked, concerned by her fresh tears.

Kristen couldn't answer. She handed him the note.

It read: "Kristen, if you are reading this, you've had an accident. Remember, it's you I love, not the car."

In a few days the fender was as good as new. Kristen, on the other hand, was better than new.

写有她姓名的字条

　　米切尔终于可以买他梦寐以求的车了。孩子们长大到已经可以自立了。克里斯蒂的车买了两年了，车型较大。他需要一辆新车，那么为什么不去实现梦想呢？

　　崭新的野马65，虽然没有什么特别的配件和电子设备，但品质是一流的，开着它上街或上班，米切尔感觉自己变年轻了，而且很酷。他盼着周末和克里斯蒂一起去郊游。

　　当然，他的心情始终充满自豪和愉悦。稍有空闲，他就会

待在车库打理和欣赏他的爱车。为之上光，四处炫耀，然而，

他至今还没有让任何人驾驶过新车。

一天下午，克里斯蒂急着去买一些东西准备晚上的派

对。可是她的车送到店里去配电脑芯片了，因芯片脱销，在等

待西海岸的补货，所以车还在店里。

克里斯蒂请米切尔开车送她去买需要的东西。而米切尔

的回答几乎让她心跳骤停。他把车钥匙交给她说："开我的车

去。我要把草坪剪完。"

"噢，不要！"她尖叫起来，"要是出点什么事怎么办？"

"亲爱的，没关系的，你会开得很好，"他说。

克里斯蒂极不情愿地钻入车内，小心翼翼地往市场开。

买全了清单上的东西，装袋工帮她把袋子放进车的后备箱。

走近后备箱时，他赞叹道："多么好的车！"

克里斯蒂一边答道："是我丈夫的车。"一边小心地驾驶

着丈夫的爱车上路了。离家只剩两个街区的时候,她有瞬间低头换收音机频道,就在那时,一条狗窜进马路。在她前面的敞蓬小货车司机猛踩刹车避开狗。她跟着紧急刹车并把方向盘向右打,但已经晚了。

她永远忘不了撞车时的巨大声响,她的车左侧保险杆撞上小货车坚硬的缓冲杠。没有人受伤,连狗也没事。但克里斯蒂几乎疯了。

"米切尔!米切尔!他永远不会原谅我,"她哭喊着。

她坐在那儿,不停地哭。货车司机走过来问她是否受伤了。

"你根本无法了解我伤得有多重,"她哭道。

"要叫救护车吗?"司机问。

稍稍控制了一下情绪,她摇摇头回答:"现在不要,等我丈夫看到他的车时一定要。"

写有她姓名的字条

货车司机自我介绍说名叫度恩,并察看了车子的损坏情况,他保证克里斯蒂的车还能开,但他需要她的保险单。

克里斯蒂打开车上的操作箱寻找保险单,狭窄的小箱内只有一个塑料封套的信袋。里面有她需要的保险单和登记证——此外还有一张写有她名字的小纸片。她很快把保险单递给度恩先生。

"这是你要的,"她说。

没再说别的话,她的注意力集中到那张写着她名字的纸片上。急于想知道上面写着什么,她迫不及待地打开它。字不多,很快就读完了。她愣住了,眼泪不停地往下流。

度恩先生看她又在流泪,很关心地问:"你真的没事吗?"

克里斯蒂无法回答,她把纸片递了过去。

上面写着:"克里斯蒂,如果你正在看这张字条,就表明你出车祸了。记住,我爱的是你,不是车。"

制造浪漫

几天后，保险杆修理如新。而另一方面，克里斯蒂的心情也焕

然一新。

Reflections . .

What special memories do you have of a time your
spouse "surprised" you with kindness?

_____

_____

_____

_____

_____

_____

_____

_____

_____

_____

_____

_____

_____

_____

_____

CHAPTER FOUR

Marking Milestones

4

注重拐点

$\mathcal{L}$earn to number your days, that you may gain a heart of wisdom. Think about good times, remember the excellent and praiseworthy moments. Let your love be sincere, as you cling to what is good. Surely goodness and mercy will follow you both all the days of your lives.

Blessing You,

your god of Every good and perfect gift

—from Psalm 90:12; Philippians 4:8; Romans 12:9; Psalm 23:6

学会规划你的生活，会让你变得更聪明。想起美好的时光和那些精彩的值得称颂的瞬间，能使你们的爱更真诚。只要你坚守那些美好的日子，仁慈和善良就会伴随你俩直到永远。

祝福你们

带给你们完美礼物的上帝

There is always something to learn about love and marriage. Every marriage has anchor points or milestones that define the relationship: people that mean a lot to us and events that change us.

Of course, the wedding itself is an important anchor point, but so is the date when you "knew" this was the one, the time you met the potential in-laws, and the moment of the proposal.

Another milestone is that first conflict that forced you into a more realistic view of each other. Your first trip as a married couple, your first Christmas, your first anniversary, your first move, and your first crisis also mark the way.

Children are anchor points of a marriage at several stages. The period of time from conception to birth is a milestone; and that's just the beginning. Children's first words, steps, school days, class programs, soccer games, weekends with grandparents, and questions about God can and should be anchor points for the marriage.

While children tend to demand our time during their growing-up years, the mar-

riage still needs special times free of their demands. Trips with other couples, marriage projects,
and anniversaries are potential anchor points in a
strong marriage.

All crisis times are milestones. Health problems,
job changes, faith struggles, and grief provide chances
for couples to pull together and offer support. Your
children's teen years are filled with one crisis after another. During these years, it's easy to take the marriage for granted and end up passing each other in
the night. A gentle hug or a walk around the block
may end up becoming an important anchor point.

To turn a moment into an anchor point for
your marriage, you need to do three things:

1. Experience the moment as a couple.

2. Talk about it. Share your joys, your sad-
ness, your pain, your fears, and your dreams.

3. Take pictures or describe the moment
in a journal or do both.

The more anchor points you have,
the more aware you become of the
value of your marriage and the
less likely you will be to cash in
such a valuable treasure.

关于爱和婚姻，有许多东西要学习。每一个婚姻都会有一些停顿点和转折点，可以诠释人们之间的关系，人本身有许多侧面，而事件可以改变我们。

当然，婚姻也是人生的重要定位点。要知道，这是你人生中唯一的日子，这一刻你得到法律的认可，还拥有那求婚的瞬间。

另一个转折点是你们之间发生第一次冲突的时候。它促使你们之间的关系更加真实，你们成为夫妻后的第一次旅行，第一次共度圣诞，第一次婚姻纪念日，第一次搬家，以及第一次遭遇危机都会留下印记。

孩子在婚姻的几个阶段也会形成转折点。

从孕育到出生，是第一个定位点，是开端。

接下来，孩子开口说第一句话，迈开第一步，开始上学，课堂学习，足球比赛，周末和祖父母在一起，有关上帝的提问等均是婚姻生活的转折点。

孩子们的成长过程，占据了我们许多

时间，夫妻还需要一些特别的自由空间，如和别的夫妻一起去旅行，重新筹划婚姻生活、结婚纪念日等都是巩固婚姻的特殊转折点。

所有危急时刻，也都是转折点。健康问题，工作问题，信任危机，悲伤时刻都可形成独特的转折点，可增强夫妻的关系，使之结合得更紧密。孩子们十几岁的时候，正是危机接踵而来之时，此时最容易淡化夫妻间的关系，夫妻间每晚的交流也会停止。一个温柔的拥抱或一起漫步小区可以帮助你们阻止更大的危机。

当婚姻生活进入拐点时，你应该做三件事：

1.夫妻双方共同度过这一时刻。

2.交谈，分享欢乐、伤心、悲痛、恐惧和梦想。

3.拍照片或写日记用以记录特别时刻。

你经历越多的转折点，就越了解你的婚姻的重要程度，就越不可能轻易放弃这无价之宝。

爱不是为相爱的日子计数——而是让其余的日子更美满。

——杰克·史密斯·沃夫曼

Love is not a matter of counting the years—it's making the years count.

—Jack Smith Wolfman

导播刚问她有什么需
要帮助时，梅利莎就忍不
住失声痛哭起来。

As soon as the counselor
asked how he could help,
Melissa began to
cry uncontrollably.

Help from strange places

Melissa didn't know where to turn. The counselor on TV seemed to have answers for others. Maybe he could help her. She was a first-time caller, and she wasn't sure what to expect. But she felt desperate, so she dialed the number. After a wait, she finally got her turn to be on the air.

As soon as the counselor asked how he could help, Melissa began to cry uncontrollably.

Between the tears, she managed to explain that she was sure her marriage was falling apart.

Her husband, Jared, was beginning to take her for granted, and she was afraid they would have a marriage in form only, without romance or oneness.

The counselor let her unburden herself for a while, then he interrupted and asked how long she and Jared had been married.

"Three weeks," she responded, embarrassed.

"Now, what has Jared done that leads you to believe that your marriage is in trouble?" asked the counselor.

Melissa let it all out. Why not? She was anonymous on the TV call-in show. "Well, as soon as he got home from work tonight, he headed straight for the hall closet and got out his bowling ball. Then he kissed me and announced that he was going bowling with some buddies from work. Why would he want to go bowling with the guys? He should want to be with me. Something's going wrong. He's already taking me for granted. I can see it now. Our marriage is over."

The counselor helped her calm down, and then he suggested that Jared was probably acting in a fairly normal manner. "Just because a couple is married doesn't mean that a spouse can take the place of all relationships. We still need friends and family. I bet he'll come home and want to tell you all about his bowling," he said.

After planting that thought, the counselor gave Melissa a task. In a little over a minute, he'd found out that before Melissa and Jared were married they had gone to a local McDonald's every Thursday evening for a special dinner. The fast-food chain would reserve them a table in the corner, and Melissa and Jared would enjoy a candlelight dinner with a white tablecloth, china plates, and silverware they had brought from home. It was a tradition they had loved. Nearby diners always thought it was especially romantic.

"Melissa," the counselor suggested, "I want you to get out all the pictures you have of when you two were dating. Select the ones that remind you of special events or special people you spent time with before you married. Also, call that McDonald's and reserve your old table for this Thursday evening. Then, take the pictures with you. After you have eaten your Big Macs, look through the pictures together and talk about the events and the people that have enriched your marriage. Can you do that?"

With renewed hope and anticipation, Melissa responded, "Yes, yes I can. Thank you."

Melissa had found just the help she needed. She couldn't wait to hang up the phone and get busy with her plans.

She and Jared didn't have many pictures, but the ones she found reminded her of several wonderful times. The pictures of other people especially drew her attention. She had been so absorbed in her new marriage that she had for-gotten how many friends they'd had before they got married. She knew it would be different now, but she made a list of the people she wanted to have lunch with and stay in touch with. Trips, adventures, crazy times, church retreats, family dinners, ball games—she had such fun reliving the memories.

Meanwhile, the TV counseling program continued. Other people were waiting for help and hope.

Then just before the closing moments of the program, Melissa was back on the line with news that she just had to share.

"Melissa, you're back. What's the problem?" asked the counselor.

Melissa was ecstatic. "Nothing! " she fairly screamed. "My husband was watching your show. Can you believe it? He was waiting for his friend to get ready for bowling, and your program was on his friend's TV. Jared called just a moment ago and told me to gather up the pictures and the china and candles. I can't believe it! He invited me to McDonald's *tonight*! "

帮助

　　梅利莎不知该怎么办，电视里咨询节目的导播正在回答问题。也许他可以帮助她。梅利莎是第一次打电话给导播，她并不知道能否解决问题。但她已绝望，只能打电话试试。等了一会儿，轮到她了。

　　导播刚问她需要什么帮助，梅利莎已经控制不住失声痛哭起来，边哭边说她的婚姻出了问题，她的丈夫杰罗德开始不爱她了，她很担心他们的婚姻只剩下躯壳，已经不存在浪漫和专一。

　　导播让她平复一下心情，然后问她和杰罗德结婚多久了。

"三个星期，"她回答时觉得很不好意思。

"那么，杰罗德究竟做了什么让你认为你们的婚姻有问题呢？"导播问。

梅利莎决定全都说出来，为什么不呢？反正她是匿名打入电视咨询节目的。"是这样的，他每晚下班回到家就径直走向客厅的衣橱，拿出保龄球亲吻我一下就说和同事们一起去打保龄球。为什么他那么愿意和同事打保龄球？他应该愿意和我待在一起。一定出了什么问题，他当我是隐身的，我算明白了，我们的婚姻完了。"

导播帮助她平静下来，然后提出自己的看法，他认为杰罗德可能通常的生活方式就是这样的，他接着说："两个人结婚了，并不代表一方可以取代另一方所有的社会关系。我们依然需要朋友和家人。我猜，他回到家，一定很想跟你谈他的保龄球。"

整理好思绪后，导播给梅利莎布置了一项工作。很短的时间里，导播已经了解到在梅利莎和杰罗德结婚前，每到星期四的晚上，都会一起去当地的麦当劳吃晚餐。这家快餐店为他们在角落保留着一个固定的位置。梅利莎会和杰罗德一起共享烛光晚餐，桌上铺着白色桌布、瓷盘，还有他们从家里带来的银餐具。这是那时他们最喜爱的约会。周围的其他就餐者都觉得非常浪漫。

"梅利莎,"导播建议说,"我想让你找出所有那些你们在一起的照片,挑选出能勾起你对结婚前一些特别的人和特别的事的回忆的照片。再打电话到那家麦当劳订下星期四晚上的老座位。然后,带上照片,在吃完麦当劳之后,一起看照片,一起谈论那些能增进你们婚姻关系的人和事,你能这么做吗?"

梅利莎感觉有了新的希望,怀着期盼的心情答道:"是的,我会这么做的,谢谢你。"

梅利莎找到的正是她需要的帮助。她迫不及待地挂上电话,忙着实施她的计划去了。

她和杰罗德没有多少照片,但她找到的那些已经足以引起一些幸福时刻的回忆。照片上其他那些人更加让她动心。她太专注于自己的婚姻,以至于忘记了他们在结婚前有那么多朋友。她知道现在不同了,她把想与其共进午餐、保持联系的人记了下来。旅行,探险,疯玩,教堂避难,家庭宴会,球赛等——她还保留着那么多鲜活的记忆。

同时,电视咨询节目还在继续。其他的人还在等着帮助,等着希望。

然而,在节目就要结束的时候,梅利莎又打入了电话,她有重要消息要和导播分享。

"梅利莎,是你吗?有什么问题吗?"导播问。

梅利莎狂喜地答道:"没有!"她几乎是在喊叫,"我丈夫看到了你们的节目。你相信吗?他当时在朋友家等待一起去打保龄球,朋友家的电视正在播你们的节目。杰罗德刚刚给我打过电话,叫我找照片,准备瓷餐具和蜡烛。我真不敢相信,他邀请我今晚去麦当劳。"

Reflections . . .

What are some of the favorite "anchor points" of your marriage? What makes them so special?

_____

_____

_____

_____

_____

_____

_____

_____

_____

_____

_____

_____

_____

_____

CHAPTER FIVE

Choosing to Be Best Friends

⑤

愿做挚友

Two are better than one. When you love one another, I live in you and My perfect love accomplishes its works in you. May love and faithfulness be essential qualities of your lives, forever written on the tablets of your hearts. Remain in My love as you wait for the mercy of Jesus Christ to bring you to eternal life!

Faithfully,

your god of love

—from Ecclesiastes 4:10–12;1 John 4:12,16;Proverbs 3:3;Jude 21

两个在一起总比一个人好，当你爱上另一个人时，我就在你心中，我完美的爱在你心中得以实现。愿爱与忠诚成为你们生命中基本的品质，永远铭刻在你们的心中。当你等待耶稣基督的仁慈带给你永生时，你将常在我的爱中常存。

忠诚的，
爱的上帝

We have casual friends, people we gather with for activities. Then there are the milestone friends, people from our past with whom we share common stories. Along the way we select a few mentor friends who inspire us and bless us and give us their wisdom. However, we have few best friends.

Best friends know each other's strengths and weaknesses. They know the secrets, and they keep the secrets. And best friends are there during crisis times. Friendship at this level requires lots of time and complete reciprocity. In other words, it's impossible to be best friends with someone who is not best friends with you.

The marriage relationship is designed to transform men and women into best friends. Although their initial attraction may have been hormonal or casual, becoming best friends gives their sexual relationship energy. Without this energy from the growing friendship, sexual intimacy will die.

Marriage has a way

of making us choose to be best friends—
or not.   Building a best-friend relationship takes both time and the willingness to risk. We can choose to let the crisis moments tear off the masks we wear, or we can allow our spouses to help us take the masks off, one layer at a time. The quicker we get past the pretension and fearfulness, the faster we can get on track to becoming best friends before a crisis hits.

When best friends are married to each other for a long time, they can finish each other's sentences. They know each other's thoughts, beliefs, and expectations. As close friends, they share feelings, intentions, goals, motives, needs, successes, and failures. When crisis times hit, we each need a trusted friend who will listen and understand and help us find what we need to deal with the crisis. That trusted friend is the one who knows us better than we know ourselves.

我们有些暂时的朋友，他们是曾经与我们共同从事某项活动的人。我们也有一些重要的朋友，他们是与我们过往人生有着共同故事的人。其中有些是我们的良师益友，他们鼓励我们、保佑我们，给我们智慧。我们还有一些最好的朋友。

最好的朋友了解彼此的长处和短处。知道对方的秘密并为之保密。最好的朋友产生在危急时刻。这个层次上的朋友需要长时间的互相关心和帮助。换句话说，就是和某个不是我的最好朋友的人，不可能成为最好的朋友。

我们把婚姻关系定义为一个男人和一个女人成为最好的朋友，尽管最初只是偶然的异性的相互吸引，成为最好的朋友可以为他们之间的关系注入新的活力。没有这种活力，他们之间的友谊和两性间的亲密关系也会消亡。

　　婚姻给了我们选择是否做最好的朋友的机会，
构建最好的朋友关系，需要我们花时间和精力去面对
危机，我们可以选择让危急时刻来揭去我们脸上的假面
具，也可以让爱人帮助我们揭去面具，每次揭去一层。我们
就能尽快摆脱各种借口和胆怯，就能在危机伤害我们之
前，尽快地成为真正的最好的朋友。

　　当好朋友伴随着婚姻度过较长时间后，他们彼此
之间已无须用语言沟通。他们相互了解对方的思
想、信仰和期望。作为亲密的朋友，他们有着共
同的情感，共同的意向，共同的目标，共同的
动机，共同的需要，共同的成功与失败。
当危机来临，我们每一个人都需要
真诚的朋友倾听、理解和帮助
我们渡过难关。真诚的朋
友了解我们胜过我
们自己。

当心灵深处最真实的
一部分在另一个心灵
中找到合适的位置，
发现奥秘……从此，
生命开始传递。

————拉里·科拉博

When the
truest part of one
soul meets the
emptiest recesses
in another and
finds something
there...life passes
from one to the
other.

—Larry Crabb

他们听到她的声音中饱含着温柔无私的爱，那是用一生的时间修炼出来的。她的年龄和脸上的皱纹是忠诚的见证。

The gentle,selfless love
they heard in her voice had
been nurtured over a
lifetime,and she proudly
wore her age and her
wrinkles as a badge
of faithfulness.

He's My Best Friend

She had been at his bedside for three days. Tired as she was, no amount of urging could convince her to go home and rest. In fact, her presence was causing scheduling problems. Suddenly, hospital staff wanted to give up days off and work extra shifts just to be around her.

There was something about her gentle spirit and her confident take on life that was infectious and somewhat angelic. She became a frequent subject of conversation at the nurses' station and in the break room. Everyone respectfully called her Mrs. Calabrese. Nurses and doctors alike took turns checking Mr. Calabrese's vitals because they wanted to talk with her.

The gentle, selfless love they heard in her voice had been nurtured over a lifetime, and she proudly wore her age and her wrinkles as a badge of faithfulness. It was clear to everyone who met Mrs. Calabrese that her best friend was the silent man whose hand she gently, constantly held. Stories about her husband flowed from her lips the moment someone entered the room. He was her lifelong investment, and they had been best friends from the beginning. Nothing had been too difficult for them to handle together. It would take years to uncover all the secrets they shared.

Once she asked a doctor who was checking her husband's chart, "Don't you think we look alike? I think so; it happens, you know."

What a rare treat it was to share a few moments

of her life.

Mr. Calabrese hadn't moved in days. His life was ebbing away as he slipped in and out of a coma. The doctors tried to prepare Mrs. Calabrese for her husband's imminent death, but she refused to listen. Her life had been intertwined with his for decades. She had helped him through scores of impossible situations, and she would help him through this one too.

Her hands were mysterious. They were timeworn and misshapen, but her slightest touch brought comfort and peace. As she sat in his room, she would not let go of Mr. Calabrese's hand. It was as though their hands belonged together. She might very well be able to baffle the medical experts and bring Mr. Calabrese home one more time.

In the middle of the night, while she slept, Mr. Calabrese suddenly awoke from his coma. Holding his hand was the bride of his youth—his best friend, the woman who had promised to love him till death.

The thought of leaving her was unbearable. Knowing death was at the door, he quietly and tenderly relished the touch of her hand for as long as he had breath. His hands had always been empty without her loving clasp. Her hands were nicked and bruised from a lifetime of working with him. Together as friends, they had traveled the uneasy road of life. So many times she had rescued him, lifted him, comforted him, and caressed him.

He couldn't bring himself to awaken her just so she could watch him die, so he wrote her a note. And he lived just long enough to finish his expression of love for his forever-faithful friend.

With only the soft glow of a bedside lamp to guide him, Mr. Calabrese used his free hand to drag a pad and pen from the table to his bed. Then, with tears running down his cheeks, he penned his message, which later became the beautiful words to the familiar song of the '50s.

Softly, I will leave you softly,

For my heart would break if you
should wake and see me go.
 So I leave you softly, long before you miss me,
Long before your arms can beg me stay
For one more hour or one more day.
After all the years, I can't bear the tears to fall.
So, I leave you softly ….

When the beep of the heart monitor signaled her husband's death, Mrs. Calabrese awoke. She was still holding her best friend's hand, though he had gone to his eternal home to await her. She noticed the verse her husband had left her, and as she read it, she thought to herself, *That's just like him. He was my best friend for life.*

他是我最好的朋友

　　她在他的床边待了整整三天了，非常疲惫，但根本不想回家去休息。事实上，她待在这里已经引起了排班的问题，因为，突然间，医院里的医护人员都为了能和她在一起而争着加班，放弃调休。

　　她身上存在的温柔体贴和坚强信念具有天使般的感染力。她是护理站和休息室里人们经常谈论的话题。每一个人都很尊敬她，称她为卡拉博力斯太太。医生和护士以同样的方式轮流帮她丈夫检查，仅仅只是为了要和她交谈一会。

他是我最好的朋友

　　他们听到她的声音中饱含着温柔无私的爱,那是用一生的时间修炼出来的。她的年龄和脸上的皱纹是忠诚的见证。很显然,每一个遇到卡拉博力斯太太的人都知道,她是那个男人,那个她一直温柔地握着他的手的安安静静的男人的最好朋友。只要有人进入房间,她就会告诉那人关于她丈夫的故事。她的丈夫是她一生的焦点,他们从一开始就是最好的朋友。什么也不能让他们分开。要了解他们之间的秘密需要许多年。

　　有一次,她问给她丈夫检查的医生:"你不认为我们长得很像吗? 我觉得是这样,要知道,这样的事真的可能发生。"

　　和她在一起待会儿也是一种独特的治疗方法。卡拉博力斯先生住院已有一段时间了, 他的生命迹象在渐渐衰退,他时而昏迷,时而清醒。

　　医生们想让卡拉博力斯太太做好思想准备,她的丈夫快要死了。但她根本不听,她的生命与她丈夫的生命缠缠绕绕几十年。她已经帮助他战胜过数次生命极限,这一次,她也要帮助他走过去。

她的手仿佛有神秘的力量。虽然它的上面布满岁月的痕迹,甚至有些变形,但她轻柔的触摸能带来舒适与平和。只要坐在丈夫病房里,她就一定紧紧握着卡拉博力斯先生的手。让人觉得他们的手是连在一起的。她极有可能打败那些医学专家,再次把卡拉博力斯先生带回家。

半夜时分,她睡着的时候,卡拉博力斯先生从昏迷中醒过来。握着他的手的人是他年轻时的新娘——他最好的朋友,承诺爱他直到死的女人。想到即将离开她,简直无法忍受。知道死神已站在门口,但只要他还在呼吸,他就会平静地、细细地感受着她的手的触感。没有她爱恋的紧握,他的手将空空如也。虽然与他一起常年劳作让她的手布满伤痕和裂痕,他们像朋友一样一起走过一段艰辛的路,然而她多次救了他,拥抱他,安慰他,宠爱他。

他是我最好的朋友

他不能叫醒她，不能让她看到死亡，因而，他写了一张字条。他活着的时间仅仅够他向他永远忠诚的朋友表达他的爱。

就着床头微弱的灯光，卡拉博力斯先生用他那只没被握住的手费力地从床头桌上拿过笔和纸。脸上滚动着热泪，写下了以下这段文字，这后来成为上世纪 50 年代最流行歌曲的最佳歌词。

悄悄地，我将离开你，

我已痛彻心扉。

请你不要醒来，看到我离开你。

在你思念我之前，我要悄悄地离去。

在你伸开双臂挽留我多待一分一秒之前，

我要悄悄地离去。

往事如烟云，热泪洒满面。

我必须悄悄地离开你。

愿做挚友

当心脏监控器发出嘟嘟的信号表明她的丈夫已经离去时，卡拉博力斯太太醒了过来。她依然握着她最好的朋友的手。虽然他已经去了天堂并在那儿等她。她看到了丈夫留给她的诗。丈夫已经离开她了。她读着诗，想着，这就是她的丈夫，她相伴终生的最好的朋友。

Reflections . . .

In what ways do you and your spouse share a "friend" relationship? How has that special dimension of love enhanced your marriage?

_____

_____

_____

_____

_____

_____

_____

_____

_____

_____

_____

_____

CHAPTER SIX

Investing

in Others

6

关爱他人

鼓励并支持彼此。让生命
充满爱,跟随我的儿子,他爱你
并会付出自己作为牺牲和祭
品。我会使你对每个人的爱不
断增加、满溢,使你富有,这样
你在任何场合都会很慷慨。

　　　　　　　光荣的,

　　　　　　　践约之神

*E*ncourage and build each other up.Live a life of love,following the example of My Son who loved you and gave Himself for you as a fragrant offering and sacrifice.I'll make your love increase and overflow for each other and for everyone else,making you rich in every way so that you can be generous on every occasion.

Gloriously,

your god of Fulfillment

—from 1 Thessalonians 5:11;Ephesians 5:2;

1 Thessalonians 3:12;2 Corinthians 9:11

One of the oft-forgotten keys to deeper intimacy is working as a team for the benefit of others.

The purpose of life is not just to build a strong marriage, but to share life with others. Nothing strengthens intimacy and oneness like getting your focus off your marriage and onto a mission.

Some couples seem to hold back, waiting for crisis moments to thrust them into some outside mission. Others allow the constant demands of parenting children to detract them from serving others. But as couples discover the secret of devoting their marriages and their families to the task of serving others, marriages in our nation will be strengthened.

More than playing together, serving together creates a sense of meaning and thankfulness.

Playing golf or tennis,

hiking, walking, running, gardening, and even dieting together are wonderful experiences, but they are all self-focused. Building a house for a deserving single mom, volunteering as camp counselors, adopting and providing for an aging widow, working together in public service, taking mission trips together, mentoring and coaching together, or counseling as a team are all others-focused.

When a couple invests in others, their focus grows beyond the needs and desires of their marriage. A serendipitous thing happens here: Hidden talents and latent strengths are uncovered. These fresh discoveries feed our appreciation and admiration of each other, and—here's the kicker—intimacy and romance are rekindled.

May your days of service bring you years of happiness!

一个可以加深我们的爱，又常常
被我们忽视的法宝就是构建一个为他人的幸福工
作的团队。

生活的目标不仅仅是巩固你的婚姻，还需与他人共
享生活。要增强爱人间的亲密关系和专一，必须把焦点从
婚姻本身转向某个使命。

有些夫妻并不是这样，他们往往要等到危机到来，
强迫他们参与到外部的某个使命中去。还有一些夫妻
强调为了养育子女所需的各种要求，而无法为他
人服务，然而，只有当这些夫妻了解到这个秘
密，即把婚姻和家庭奉献到为他人服务的
工作中去，婚姻才可以牢不可破。

比起一起游玩，共同为别
人服务可以创造出一种富
有意义、令人感动的
意境。

一起打高尔夫、网球、远足、散步、跑步、园艺或一起吃饭都是非常好的活动，但那是以自我为中心的。而为单身妈妈建造房屋，自愿充当野营的顾问，收养或供养年老的寡妇，一起参与公共服务工作，组织团队旅行，提供指导和培训，从事咨询服务等都是以他人为中心的活动。

当一对夫妻投身到为他人服务中去，他们就不会只关心自己婚姻的需要和愿望。于是，就发生了这样的事：他们被埋藏的智慧和潜在的能量被释放出来。这些新的刺激让夫妻双方更加欣赏和赞赏对方，因而已经失去的亲密与浪漫又会被重新点燃了。

为他人服务吧，让你们的生活更幸福！

爱是在面对生
活中的危难，从而
重新认识对方中
成长的。

——约翰·度登

love thinves
in the face of all
life's hagards,
save one—neglect.

—John Dryden

He pointed to her and
mouthed the words,
"I love you."

他对她说出神圣的"我爱你"。

The Tornado's Silver Lining

The honeymoon was a dream, and after the first month of "playing house," Rick and Cindi thought their honeymoon might last forever. Then came the unthinkable.

They heard the warnings on television and radio, urging people to go to the safest rooms of their homes. The sirens blasted that irritating tone that rattles walls.

Cindi had never been through a tornado warning, and she was terrified. Rick had matter-of-factly gathered blankets and pillows, throwing them into the bathtub. Cindi's grip on his arm tightened as

they closed the bathroom door.   Once Rick had arranged the blankets and pillows,   they both climbed
into the tub,   pulled the blankets over themselves,
and with their arms wrapped around each other,
waited.   By then they could hear the distant roar,
which grew louder by the second.

It sounded as if the tornado were cutting a path
right through their first-floor apartment.   They were
smothered by the roar of wind.   Then the intensity
began to fade,   and they experienced an eerie
silence.

With the blanket still draped around their shoul-
ders, they opened the bathroom door, expecting the
adjoining room to be gone—but nothing had
changed.   Cindi's Coke glass was still on the kitchen
counter. The dirty dishes were still in the sink; even
the morning paper was still spread across the table.
But when they opened their front door,   reality hit
hard.   The scene from their doorway could have
come from the cutting-room floor of *Twister*.   They
saw empty lots across the street where their neigh-
bors' houses had stood.   Vehicles were scattered

everywhere; paper, clothes, splintered two-by-fours; and uprooted trees jumbled together as though someone had mixed an odd, giant tossed salad. Then came the sounds—cries for help, moans, screams, barking dogs, and distant sirens.

Rick noticed that Cindi was no longer sobbing. She had the look of confident determination that a woman gets when she knows exactly what has to be done and how to do it. They both got to work immediately, and their apartment became the center of operations.

Rick helped in the search and rescue, while Cindi comforted the hurting and handed out supplies, including every blanket, pillow, and towel they owned—even the shower gifts they had decided to return. They gave their bed to the family of six down the block. Cindi tirelessly provided food, water, and hot coffee for the workers, while Rick pulled people from the disaster. They were both running on adrenaline.

During a short break, Rick returned to the apartment for a drink of water. There he saw his new wife, unaware of his presence, comforting Mrs. Thomas, who had lived in the big two-story house on the corner. Everything Mrs. Thomas owned, even her yappy little poodle, had disappeared. Mrs. Thomas sat in shock over her loss, and Cindi listened attentively to her pain. She cared deeply about the woman and her devastation. Even in the horror of these moments, nothing seemed to daunt Cindi's spirit.

Finally, Rick got her attention—just a glance and a message. He pointed to her and mouthed the words, "I love you."

Shortly after Rick's visit, Cindi caught a glimpse of him helping to pull a half-buried ten-year-old girl from beneath a pile of shattered wall and broken tree limbs. As the youngster hugged Rick, Cindi's eyes flooded with pride. "That's my husband out there," Cindi muttered to no one. "Thank you, God!

Thank you for Rick. Keep him safe," she prayed. God was listening.

That night when Rick and Cindi lay on their bare floor to sleep, they were wrapped in each other's arms, not because they were still "playing house," not because they were afraid to let go of each other, and not because they were cold. Rick and Cindi were wrapped in each other's arms because, for them, this was a holy moment. They had found a new level of closeness by doing something for others. As Rick and Cindi came near to losing everything they had, they discovered a new treasure for their marriage.

龙卷风的银衬里

蜜月宛如梦，一个月轻松甜蜜的生活后，罗克和欣蒂觉得他们的蜜月一去不复返了。而此时，发生了一件意想不到的事。

广播和电视里发出警报，要人们藏到家里最安全的房间里去。刺耳的警笛声连绵不断。

欣蒂从来没经历过旋风警报，她很害怕。罗克平静地抓起几床毛毯和枕头扔到浴缸里。欣蒂紧紧抓住他的胳膊，关上了浴室的门。罗克铺好毛毯和枕头，他俩一起爬进浴缸，拉过毛毯盖在身上，两人紧紧拥抱在一起，等着。他们听到远处风的吼叫声，而且越来越响。

听起来，旋风的路线正是他们那一层的公寓。呼啸的风声让他们几乎窒息。继而，强度开始减弱，四周一片寂静。

裹着毯子，打开了浴室的门，以为相邻的房间已经不见了，但什么也没有改变，欣蒂的可乐杯还在厨房的灶台上。脏盘子还在水池里。甚至早报还摊开在餐桌上。但当他们打开大门，发现破坏惊人。门道连着地板已扭曲断裂的房间。他们看到街道对面空空的一片废墟，那儿原来是邻居的房屋。车辆散落得到处都有。报纸、衣服、各种碎片，七零八落的，混杂着被连根拔起的大树，仿佛搅拌着巨大而怪异的晃动的色拉。接着传来各种声响——呼救声，呻吟声，尖叫声，狗吠声和远处的警笛声。

罗克发现欣蒂已不再哭泣，她看起来已经下定决心，此刻她知道究竟该做什么、怎么做。他们立即开始工作，他们的房间成为救助中心。

罗克帮助搜寻和营救，欣蒂安慰伤者，分发救助品，包括他们所有的毛毯、枕头，还有自己用的毛巾——甚至那些准备回送给朋友的大量礼物。他们把床也送给了离此六个街区的一户人家。欣蒂不知疲倦地为工作的人准备食物、水、热咖啡，而罗克也在灾难中救人。两人都非常投入。

稍事休息，罗克回到家里喝水。看到了他的新娘。她正在安慰托马斯太太，没有注意到他。托马斯太太住在街角的一座两层楼的房子里，现在所有的东西都化为乌有，连那只爱叫的狮子狗都没有了。她受到打击，坐在那儿伤心地述说。欣蒂全神贯注地倾听着，非常关心她的损失和悲痛。即使在这种悲伤时刻，欣蒂依然精神振奋。

最后，她终于看见罗克了，仅仅看了一眼，打了个招呼。罗克对着她说："我爱你。"

罗克走后不久，欣蒂一眼看到罗克正从一堆倒塌的墙和树木的断枝下抢救一个埋住半个身子的 10 岁小女孩。当获救的小女孩拥抱着罗克时,欣蒂的眼中充满骄傲。"那是我丈夫,"欣蒂自言自语地嘀咕,"谢谢你,上帝,请你保佑罗克,保佑他安全。"

那天晚上,罗克和欣蒂躺在光光的地板上睡觉,他们双臂相拥着,不是因为蜜月中的游戏,不是因为害怕对方离开,也不是因为冷。紧紧相拥是因为,对他们来说,这是神圣的时刻。他们发现了增进亲密感情的新方法,那就是关爱他人。罗克和欣蒂在几乎失去一切时却找到了他们婚姻中新的珍宝。

Reflections . .

What special times of ministering to others have you and your spouse shared? How have these experiences enriched your relationship?

_____

_____

_____

_____

_____

_____

_____

_____

_____

_____

_____

_____

_____

_____

CHAPTER SEVEN

Finding Forgiveness

7

寻求谅解

$\mathscr{B}$e subject to one another in the fear of Christ. Above all, love each other deeply, because love covers over a multitude of faults and differences. Forgive the grievances you are holding against each other; let love bind the hurtful wounds. Let My Son's peace rule in your hearts as I continue to build your house.

My Enduring Love and Commitment,
your god of Restoration

—from Ephesians 5:21; 1 Peter 4:8; Colossians 3:13–16;
Psalms 127:1; 138:8

在对基督的敬畏中服从彼此。首先，深爱彼此，因为爱会覆盖所有缺点与差异。原谅彼此之间的抱怨不平，让爱来约束伤害。让我和平法则长存你心。

我永恒的爱与承诺
恢复之神

Betrayal may be the most painful emotion to deal with; the pain it brings certainly creates long-lasting hurt. It can come in many shapes: infidelity, deceit, disloyalty, dishonesty. The out-come is the same—undermined trust, emotional torment, and thoughts of retaliation. We have probably all heard people say that they just don't seem able to forgive, as though they had some genetic defect that physically prevents them from forgiving. But in marriage, forgiveness is not an option; it is a necessity.

To forgive means that we choose to give up the right to hurt the one who has hurt us. It is a conscious choice. To make that choice, however, we must be aware of the pain. That's why so many counselors ask clients to journal, to write out the hurt inflected by the offender. Acknowledging and describing these painful memories is the first step in dealing constructively with the hurt. Once the true feelings are out in the open, forgiveness becomes possible.

Granted, it's tough for us to forget past wrongs; only God can do that. But we can pardon the guilt and refuse to keep punishing the offender. When we give up the right to hurt the one who has hurt us, we grant the offender the grace to start over. When powered by forgiveness, unbelievable transformations can occur.

Forgiveness is the most unique concept to come from the Christian faith. When God forgives us, He forgets the guilt and the sin. His forgiveness empowers us to begin again. He doesn't trap us or label us or gripe at us; He removes the failure and encourages us to try again.

When we truly understand God's forgiveness, we will be more eager to forgive others.

The choice is ours.

背叛也许是最悲伤的难以应对的情绪，可以造成长期的伤害。它以多种形式表现出来，如虚假、欺骗、不忠、不实等。而结果都是一样的——破坏信任、情感受伤及伺机报复。我们经常听到人们说他们不可能谅解什么。因为他们先天的个性不允许。然而，如果是夫妻，谅解对方是必然的，没有选择的余地。

谅解意味着我们放弃了反击伤害过我们的人的权利，是个理性的选择。然而，我们必须完全了解受到伤害的程度，才能做出选择。这也是为什么许多咨询专家要求客户写日记，记下遇到背叛后的心情变化。勇于承认并描述这些悲愤的记忆，是迈向理性对待的第一步。一旦打开了真诚的情感

之门,谅解就会接踵而来。然而,事
实是要忘掉以往的伤害是困难的, 只有神仙才能
办到。但如果我们能够原谅伤害过我们的人不去惩罚
他,我们放弃了惩罚的权利,我们宽恕了他,文明就得以
延续。从而也让我们获得力量,难以置信的改变就可能发
生。

饶恕是我们最基本的信念,当我们向上帝乞求饶
恕时,他原谅了我们的过失和陋习。让我们可以重
新开始。没有戏弄,指使和控制他赶走挫败,
鼓励我们重新努力。

当我们真正了解了饶恕的意
义,我们就更愿意原谅他人。

如何选择全在自
己。

維持一段幸
福的夫妻以方懂
得寬恕。

Marriages
that last involve
the union of two
good forgivers.

—unknown

Everything in her apartment began to remind her of treasured moments with Tom.

窝所内的每样东西都让她回想起与汤姆一起度过的珍贵时光。

The Relationship Resurrection

Tom was clueless and stunned.

They'd had some rocky moments at first, but over the last few years, everything had seemed to settle down. In fact, Tom had recently commented to a friend that he and Rhonda were about to celebrate twenty-five years of marriage and that things had never been better.

"We really understand each other," he'd said.

That's why Rhonda's note was so shocking. Surely it was a terrible joke! It must be a joke. But it was not.

Tom quickly surveyed the house only to discover that all traces of Rhonda had disappeared. Pictures and knickknacks, clothes and personal items, china and silver, even the old rocker she had inherited from her grandmother—Rhonda had taken everything connected to her. He looked at the note again as his shock turned to anger.

"Tom, I'm tired of pretending. Our marriage is dead. Don't try to find me. The divorce papers will be served tomorrow. Just sign them, and let's bury this dead relationship. Rhonda."

Never, not even for one moment, had Tom considered that he and Rhonda had serious problems, much less that they would get divorced. How could he have been so blind? How could she have been so unhappy and not talked to him? The sting of her deception, punctuated by the painful finality of the divorce decree, left Tom drained, distrusting, and cynical.

In spite of the comfort his friends offered him and the devoted support of his two grown children, Tom pulled away, withdrawing from those close to him and losing himself in work.

While Tom wandered the maze of doubt and despair, his friends and family continued to ask God for a miracle—a resurrected marriage.

As the divorce became final and for months afterward, Rhonda began to seriously question her actions. Everything in her apartment began to remind her of treasured moments with Tom. God began peeling the blindness away from her eyes. She had discarded the most treasured part of her life. After all, Tom had in his own way, and sometimes without his knowledge, helped her to become who she was. In fact, he was the one who had encouraged her to try new things. He had instilled in her a confidence that she had turned against him. He was far from perfect, but so was she. Could she get Tom back? Could the love that had died be resurrected?

It took several phone conversations before Tom agreed to meet Rhonda for coffee. Although Rhonda was unassuming and penitent, Tom struggled. He couldn't see beyond his pain, but his pain meant there was still hope.

After several discussions, and with the encouragement of their kids, Tom and Rhonda began attending a marriage-therapy group. At first they felt like misfits—after all, they were divorced—but they soon discovered their issues were the same as the others'. These couples were struggling with power and control, communication and conflict, trust and expectations — just like Tom and Rhonda. With the help of the counselor, they were working on their differences. Tom and Rhonda often found themselves offering warnings against divorce as a solution. After each session Tom and Rhonda talked for hours. As time passed, Tom felt his pain diminishing and being replaced by a willing forgiveness.

Then after an ordinary evening of group sharing and relationship building, Tom announced he had a question. With five unsuspecting couples giving him their full attention, he turned to Rhonda and asked, "Rhonda, will you honor me by becoming my wife, again?"

Rhonda shouted, "Yes, oh yes! "

The next time the marriage-therapy group met, a strange thing happened. Instead of spending their time discussing issues and problems, these new friends joined with Tom and Rhonda's children in a resurrection ceremony. Tom and Rhonda were married again, but this time the vows joined a man and a woman who were fully aware of the meaning of "for better or for worse." They had been to both edges of marriage, and now they could talk about it.

复婚

汤姆事先一无所知,他几乎晕厥。

他们开始的时候是不太顺,但这些年来,一切仿佛都解决了。事实上,汤姆最近还对朋友提起他要和萝恩达庆祝二十五周年结婚纪念。那是再好不过的事了。

"我们真的很了解对方,"他那时说。

这就是萝恩达的字条让他如此震惊的原因。简直是一个残酷的玩笑。要是玩笑就好了,但不是。

汤姆迅速搜索整个屋子,寻找萝恩达离家出走的痕迹。照片和各种小玩意,衣服和个人用品,瓷盘和银器,甚至她外婆留给她的破旧的摇椅——凡是与萝恩达有关的东西,一样不剩全带走了。他再次看那张字条,震惊变为愤怒。

"汤姆,我不想再假装下去。我们的婚姻已经完了。不要找我,离婚协议书明天送到,签名就行。让我们埋葬这段已经死亡的感情。萝恩达。"

从来也没有,汤姆一次也没有想到他和萝恩达之间有什么严重的问题。更没有想过离婚。他怎么如此愚钝。为什么她过得如此不快乐却从没有告诉过他。这种欺骗刺伤了他,惨痛的离婚结局刺伤了他。汤姆感到筋疲力尽,难以置信而且愤世不公。

尽管朋友们都安慰他,帮他照顾两个孩子,汤姆还是选择躲避,躲避那些亲近他的人,躲避到繁忙的工作中去。

在汤姆迷惘、疑虑而绝望时,他的朋友和家人却不断地在乞求奇迹的发生——复婚。

离婚几个月后,萝恩达开始认真地反思自己的行为。居所内的每一件东西都开始让她想起和汤姆在一起时的珍贵时刻。她的盲目被一层层地剥开。她明白了她放弃的是她一生最宝贵的一段时光。总之,汤姆以他自己的方式,不光是用知识,帮助她成为现在的萝恩达。事实上,正是他鼓励萝恩达去尝试新的事物,潜移默化地让她有了离开他的信心。他虽然不完美,但自己也一样。能不能挽回汤姆?已死亡的爱情能

复婚

否重生？

萝恩达打了好几个电话，汤姆才答应一起喝咖啡。尽管萝恩达真诚地悔过，汤姆还是很矛盾。他无法摆脱受伤的心情，他的伤心也表明了希望尚存。

几度磋商后，在孩子们的鼓励下，汤姆和萝恩达一起参加了一个婚姻心理治疗活动。开始他们不适应——毕竟他们已不是夫妻——但，很快他们发现，他们的情况跟其他人一模一样。这些夫妻均在权利与控制，交流与冲突，现实与期望中痛苦挣扎——就像汤姆和萝恩达一样。在指导顾问的帮助下，他们认真地对待这些分歧。他们发现自己常常告诫自己离婚不应该是结局。每一次聚会后，汤姆和萝恩达都要交谈很长时间。随着时间的流逝，汤姆觉得他内心的伤痛渐渐减少，越来越可以容得下谅解了。

在经过一段时间晚上共同参加小组活动及重建关系后，汤姆宣布了一个消息。五对相互信任的夫妻现场为他的话作见证，他转向萝恩达说："萝恩达，我可以荣幸地再次成为你的丈夫吗？"

萝恩达大声喊道："当然，当然可以！"

接下来的那次婚姻治疗小组的聚会，发生了一件不平常的事。他们没有像平时那样讨论各种状况和问题。这些新的朋友还有汤姆和萝恩达的孩子们一起举办了一场复婚仪式。汤姆和萝恩达再次成为夫妻。而这次,婚礼上宣誓的双方都非常明白"有福同享,有难同当"的深刻含义。他们都曾走到婚姻的边缘。现在他们已经不再惧怕提起它。

Reflections . . .

How has the power of forgiveness blessed your marriage?